The Old Woman's Cat

By Alice Lesak

Illustrated by Stephanie Koller

PALMETTO
PUBLISHING
Charleston, SC
www.PalmettoPublishing.com

First Edition

Hardcover ISBN: 979-8-8229-3365-1
Paperback ISBN: 979-8-8229-3386-6

Once there was a dog named Katie who lived with an old woman in a cottage in the woods. They were very happy and did everything together.

They walked in the woods together.

They played ball together.

They ate their meals together.

And at night they slept in the old woman's bed together.

One lovely, crisp autumn day, when Katie and the old woman came home from their morning walk in the woods, there was a box on the front steps.

"I wonder what that could be," said the old woman. Katie sniffed it and listened to it. She didn't know what it was, but she knew it was alive! She was very excited and couldn't help bouncing up and down on her front legs as the old woman picked up the box and opened it.

"My goodness!" said the old woman as she reached inside. Very carefully she lifted out a tiny, little kitten. "Who could have left you here?" It was a rather funny looking kitten. His fur wasn't quite black, and it wasn't quite brown, and it stuck out in all directions. Then Katie heard the kitten begin to purr. She liked the way it sounded. The old woman put the kitten against her chest, and the kitten snuggled into her neck. He purred and he purred. "Well aren't you the sweetest little thing!" the old woman declared. "Let's get you inside where it's warm and get you something to eat."

Katie and the old woman took the kitten inside where the old woman warmed some milk and set the bowl and the kitten on the kitchen table. The kitten lapped up all the milk. Then he walked over to the old woman so she could pick him up and cuddle him. "My goodness, you were hungry!" The old woman looked at Katie and said, "I think I'll call him Jake. What do you think?" Katie wagged her tail to let the old woman know she approved.

The old woman carefully held Jake out for Katie to smell. "He's very small and you're very big. You'll have to be careful with him. He's too little to play with you. You'll have to wait until he gets bigger for that." Katie sniffed Jake, and Jake sniffed Katie. Jake began to purr again, and Katie began to wag her tail again, and the old woman knew that Katie would be careful with Jake. Katie was a good dog.

As Jake grew, Katie tried to teach him the rules. Katie told him, "Don't play with the toilet paper."

Jake didn't listen.

Katie told him, "Don't climb the pantry shelves."

Jake didn't listen.

Over the winter, Jake started growing from a fuzzy, little kitten into a handsome, black cat with thick fur and a bushy, black tail. But Jake always thought he was bigger and smarter and more grown up than he really was. And when Katie tried to tell him he shouldn't do something, Jake thought he knew better than Katie did, and he always did whatever he wanted when Katie wasn't watching.

One day, when Katie and the old woman were taking a walk
in the woods, Katie heard something behind them. She
turned around and saw Jake following them, tail held high,
and quite pleased with himself. When the old woman saw
Katie looking behind them, she looked too. "Well, my
goodness! Jake, did you think you wanted to take a walk with
us? How lovely!" Jake fluffed himself out with fur that was
starting to turn thick and black, and he was very proud of
himself. From that day on, whenever Katie and the old
woman took a walk in the woods, Jake went with them.

One day, as they were walking in the woods, Jake saw a path they had never taken. It looked interesting, and he wanted to explore it. But as soon as he started down the path, Katie told him, "Don't go down that path."

"Why not?" Jake asked.

"Because a fox lives in a hollow tree down that path."

"So what?" Jake asked, not happy that Katie was trying to tell him what to do again.

"A hungry fox could catch you and eat you," Katie told him.

As always, Jake didn't believe her. He thought, "I can run very fast, and I can climb a tree, and no fox is ever going to catch me." But he didn't say anything. He just followed Katie and the old woman until they got back to the cottage.

But as soon as Katie and the old
woman went inside, Jake turned
around and headed back to the path
that Katie told him not to go down. It
looked like it would be so much fun to
explore.

Jake took his time as he made his way along the path. He sniffed the ferns and the little red berries that grew on small, green plants close to the ground.

And he hid under a fire bush to watch a woodpecker making a hole in a rotten tree so it could find a bug to eat. Jake thought he could catch that woodpecker, but before he even got all the way out from under the fire bush, the woodpecker had flown away.

Jake heard insects buzzing and birds chirping.

And when he passed a big pond, he was startled when a beaver swimming nearby slapped her big, flat tail on the water, and it made a loud, cracking sound.

Jake was having a wonderful time, and he completely forgot about the fox as he approached an interesting, fallen log… until he saw, out of the corner of his eye, a flash of red fur racing towards him! He barely had time to climb the big pine tree beside him, and he climbed it faster than he had ever climbed in his life!

The fox jumped against the tree's trunk and growled and made a funny sound that wasn't at all like Katie's bark or a squirrel's angry chattering or anything else Jake had ever heard. But Jake didn't laugh. He knew the fox was deadly serious. Jake just wanted to stay as far away from the fox as he could. He crawled out on a big branch and lay there, holding tight with his claws and watching until the fox finally stopped jumping against the tree's trunk. Eventually, the fox turned away and headed back up the path.

Jake stayed up on the branch of the big pine tree for a very long time after the fox disappeared into the woods. He waited until his heart was no longer beating too fast and his body was no longer shaking. Then he climbed back down the big pine tree and went home.

Jake joined Katie and the old woman whenever they went for a walk in the woods together, or played ball together, or ate their meals together. And at night they all slept in the old woman's bed together. Jake loved to snuggle against Katie when they slept. But sometimes Katie got too warm with Jake's hot body pressed tight against her. Then she would get up and move to a different part of the bed. When that happened, Jake moved too, and he snuggled against the old woman and purred with contentment.

One day, when Jake was sitting in the shade of the big oak tree behind the cottage, he heard something moving through the ferns and bushes behind him. Jake now thought of himself as a big, grown-up cat that wasn't afraid of anything. So he waited and watched, and soon an animal that was just about the same size as Jake came walking out of the woods. The animal had red fur and a bushy, red and black tail with a white tip.

"Hi," the little animal said to Jake. "Who are you?"

"I'm Jake," Jake told him. "Who are you?'

"I'm Herbie," the little animal said.

"Are you a fox?" Jake asked.

"I am," said Herbie.

"What are you doing here?" Jake asked.

"Looking for someone to play with," Herbie replied. "Do you want to play?"

"I think it's safer for me to stay away from foxes," Jake told him, remembering his narrow escape from the big fox near the hollow log.

"But I don't have anyone to play with," Herbie protested. "Won't you play with me?"

Jake hesitated. Herbie was a little fox. Jake didn't think
Herbie could hurt him. And Jake was sure he could run
faster than Herbie if he needed to. "Come on," said
Herbie, lying down and rolling over playfully. "Come
play." He rolled over again, moving quite close to Jake.
Then he reached out his paw and tapped Jake's paw.
Jake lifted his paw and tapped Herbie's paw back.

Soon Jake was rolling around on the ground with Herbie. Then they were chasing each other around the big oak tree. "You can't catch me," Herbie yelled as he ran off into the woods.

"Oh yes I can!" Jake yelled back as he ran after Herbie. They ran through the ferns and crossed a log that had fallen across a small stream and continued on through a small clearing where daisies grew in the grass.

All afternoon Jake
and Herbie chased each
other through the woods,
laughing and running and
rolling together on the ground.
Grasshoppers jumped away from them.
Red squirrels in the trees chattered and
scolded them. And they startled two
mourning doves that
flew away as soon as
they saw Jake and
Herbie heading
toward them.

Finally, when Jake and Herbie were both tired, they sat down and rested. But a few minutes later, Herbie started looking around, and then he started to look scared. "What's wrong?" asked Jake.

"I don't know where we are," Herbie said, looking like he might start to cry. "I don't know how to get home."

Jake looked around and knew exactly where they were. He had walked all over these woods with Katie and the old woman. "Don't worry," Jake told Herbie. "I'll help you." But Jake wasn't quite sure how. If Herbie didn't know where he lived, how would Jake ever find Herbie's home?

Then Jake thought about the hollow log where the big fox had chased him, and he suddenly understood that the big fox was trying to keep Jake away from her baby, Herbie. "Do you live in the hollow log with the really big fox?" Jake asked Herbie.

"I do,"Herbie said.

"That big fox is my mom."

"Then I know how to get you home," Jake said. "Come on."

Jake led the way, and Herbie followed. They passed by
where they had startled the two mourning doves and made
the red squirrels in the trees chatter and scold them and
where they made the grasshoppers jump away from them.
They ran back through the small clearing where the daisies
grew in the grass and went back over the log that had fallen
across the small stream. They ran back through the ferns,
and suddenly they were back at the big oak tree behind the
old woman's little cottage in the woods.

From there Jake led Herbie to the trail that Katie had told Jake never to go down. They passed more ferns and walked by the red berries that grew on tiny green plants close to the ground. They passed the fire bush where Jake had hidden while he watched the woodpecker make a hole in the rotten tree. They heard insects buzzing and birds chirping as they passed the pond where the beaver had slapped her big, flat tail against the water, making a loud, cracking sound that startled Jake the first time Jake passed by. Jake knew they were getting close to where Herbie lived … and where his mother lived.

"I think I better leave now before your mother sees me," Jake said. "Do you know where you are?"

"It's my home!" Herbie cried in excitement. "You brought me home!"

"You'll be okay now. See you later," Jake said, and he turned around and ran back down the trail before Herbie's mother saw him.

The next afternoon, Jake was back under the big oak tree behind the old woman's little cottage. He heard rustling in the ferns and bushes behind him, then Herbie came walking out of the woods. Jake was happy to see his friend … until he saw Herbie's mother coming out of the woods behind him. Jake didn't wait. He was up the big oak tree before Mama fox's tail made it out of the ferns after her.

"Don't run away," Mama fox said. "I won't hurt you." Jake didn't say anything. He wasn't taking any chances with Mama fox. "Herbie told me he got lost and you brought him home," Mama fox said. Jake still didn't say a word.

"I'm more grateful than I can say." Mama fox sat down, hoping she might not seem so scary to Jake. "And I came here in person to tell you that Herbie has my permission to come and play with you every day, as long as you walk him home before it gets dark."

Herbie was jumping up and down with excitement. "Isn't that great, Jake? We can play together every day!"

"I don't know," Jake said. "How do I know you aren't trying to trick me?" he asked Mama fox.

Herbie was rolling over and over then jumping up and down again, he was so excited. "It's not a trick," he insisted. "Please come down. Please, please, please!"

Mama fox lowered her head, looked at the ground, and Jake could hear in her voice that her words were sincere. She said, "I want my boy to be happy. Playing with you makes him happy. Please Jake, please come down and play with him."

Finally, Jake took a chance. Very cautiously he came down from the branch in the big oak tree, ready to run back up if Mama fox moved a muscle. But she didn't. "Come on," Herbie shouted as he started to run around the tree. "Chase me! Chase me! Chase me!" Mama fox nodded her head in permission.

Herbie stopped running and hid behind the tree. Very carefully, Jake turned back to Mama fox and stretched his neck to look behind the tree. "Boo!' shouted Herbie, jumping out from behind the tree. Jake jumped, startled. Then he couldn't help himself. Jake liked to play as much as Herbie did. He started chasing Herbie around the tree as Mama fox smiled, watching her baby playing with a cat.

Katie and the old woman happened to look out the sliding doors at the back of the cottage to see Jake playing with a baby fox while Mama fox sat nearby and watched in approval. "Well, will you look at that, Katie?" The old woman said in amazement. Katie did look at that. She saw Jake playing with a fox, and she just shook her head.

Milton Keynes UK
Ingram Content Group UK Ltd.
UKHW050205211123
432956UK00002B/68